Coming Storm

An Adventure from
The Quest for Truth

Imagined and Written By
Brock Eastman

Illustrated By
Brandon Dorman

Dedication

To my cousin Jessica:

Believe it or not you inspired quite a bit of Obbin.

My partner in mischief; family parties wouldn't have
been near as fun without you.

Love you Messers and thanks for serving our country.

Table of Contents

PREFACE

Coming Storm was written as a story for the January 2012 issue of Clubhouse® magazine. It's supplemental to Taken; the first book in The Quest for Truth series. This edition has been expanded beyond the story that was featured in Clubhouse magazine, but includes the art found in the story.

The *Coming Storm* was written from Obbin's perspective, and gives his viewpoint on the first time he met the Wikk twins, Mason and Austin. The Quest for Truth is a five book series following the Wikk kids, who must rescue their parents from an evil group of soldiers called the Übel.

The wonderful illustrations were created by Brandon Dorman, who also has done the covers for the other books in The Quest for Truth series.

The Quest for Truth Series:
Taken
Risk
Unleash
Tangle
Hope

Other books by Brock Eastman:
Sages of Darkness series:
HowlSage
BlizzardSage
CrimsonSage

The Imagination Station Series:
Showdown with the Shepherd
Challenge on the Hill of Fire

SURE SHOT

Green leaves still covered the trees. Lush ferns swayed, giving no hint to the ice storm that was about to strike Jahr des Eises. Obbin's tiny planet was beautiful, but also known for its brutal winters.

Obbin had just a few hours left before he would be cooped up between the high valley walls of Cobalt Gorge until the next thaw. That was why he and his brother, Rylin, had escaped over their secret vine rope bridge. The winter storm known as Eises came once every two years, locking his home into a yearlong ice prison.

Obbin skipped down the well worn dirt path he and his brother always used. He couldn't see the sky through the thick canopy of leaves, but in a few short minutes he'd have an amazing view.

Rylin and Obbin had built a fort in a sturdy oak tree. The upper floor of the tree house sat inches above the topmost leaves, more than three hundred feet up. The brothers stopped 100 feet from the tree's location and looked at each other. Obbin knew the challenge that Rylin was about to announce.

"First one to release the ladder wins," Rylin said. "On the count of three."

Obbin smiled brightly. "You're on."

"One, two, three!"

The brothers dashed forward. Rylin bumped Obbin with his elbow, pushing him off the path—but it did nothing to slow him down. Obbin hopped over a large fern and was right back on the trail.

Rylin's strides were longer. The older brother arrived at the tree first, pulling out his slingshot and dropping down to search for a stone.

Obbin took out his own slingshot, screeching to a halt and digging into the deep side pockets of his fur shorts for one of the many pebbles he kept handy. He took out a stone and rolled it in his blue hand for a moment.

With the pebble loaded in the leather strap, Obbin pulled back and aimed at his target, a lever that would release the rope ladder needed to access the tree fort.

"Three, two, one," Obbin called aloud. His fingers released the leather. *Plink.* The stone hit its mark.

Shoomp, shoomp, shoomp. The rope ladder dropped from a branch and unrolled, the end landing at Obbin's feet.

"Victory!" he called.

Rylin shook his head. "You won't win next time," he said. "But since you did, you get to go up first."

For Obbin that was a true reward. Rylin always claimed he got to go up the tree first, because he was the one that had discovered the secret way out of the gorge.

Obbin started up the tree. "See you at the top."

The vine-rope ladder was twenty feet in length, taking him only to the lowest level of the tree house. The first floor wasn't much. A narrow set of planks, barely wide enough to stand on. The idea was the fort should be as inconspicuous as possible to any who might be wandering the great woods.

From there small notches were wedged out of the tree trunk itself, and only with bare feet could one grip the notches and ascend to the next level. More than thirty feet up the tree, the second floor was a welcoming destination. The platform extended out across several large branches. Three huts had been built-Rylin's, Obbin's and a food storage room.

The brothers often snuck out from Cobalt gorge and spent the nights here in the tree house. Obbin knew their parents never assumed they'd left the safety of the gorge, but were camping somewhere in the jungle that covered the valley walls.

A sturdy ladder extended to the next floor, which had several rope bridges extending from it to other nearby trees. The fourth, fifth, and sixth floors, each held cages of creatures the boys had captured throughout the two years of fair weather. Those cages all had been emptied now, the animals released back into the woods, or smuggled into the gorge to be kept as pets.

The seventh level was the halfway point up the height of the tree. This floor had the largest of all huts. Rylin had named it the Lodge. An assorted collection of items had been salvaged from the castle and brought here. The task of getting it up the tree had been a great deal of pulling on vine-ropes by Obbin and Rylin. It took nearly three weeks to get all the things up into the Lodge; two chairs, a telescope and tripod, a large silver bowl for fires, a low square table, and three huge barrels that were used to collect rain water for a homemade shower.

From there it was another very long climb, to the last four levels. These floors were far smaller than all but the first. At most, they might be able to fit half a dozen people on one, but then it became a question of the strength of the branches. Besides that, only two people knew of the tree fort's existence. Only the topmost platform had been reinforced with extra poles.

Rylin called this the Nest. From there they could look out far across the forest. They could see the mountains in which rested their home. A castle nestled deep beneath the protective cloak of blue steam. They could also see as far as the shiny dome; a city covered by a massive half-globe of glass and metal. The brothers had never attempted to go to this city, for they'd seen the soldiers on flying things before.

On a clear day, smoke trails rising from the city of rejection could be seen. Rylin and Obbin had once visited this collection of rundown buildings. It was easy to slip into the village. There were no stone paved streets like in their city, or any sort of organization to the buildings and paths, just a haphazard jumble of wooden and rusting metal buildings. They'd never returned after a terribly frightening incident with a lizard.

CRASH LANDING

A sea of green treetops stretched out before Obbin and Rylin. They stood on the uppermost landing of the tree house. Dark purple winter clouds boiled in the distance, slowly choking off the sunlight and covering the forest in shadow.

Rylin sighed. "Well, brother, it won't be long now. We'd better get going. If the storm hits, crossing the vine bridge will become dangerous."

"Doesn't scare me." Obbin frowned.

"Nothing scares you." Rylin put his arm around his brother's shoulder. "Except being bored. I promise we'll venture out into the snow at least once."

"Yes, but it's not the same as seeing the forest alive and green," Obbin complained. "And we have to wear those thick, itchy coats you made."

The brothers had never been assigned any winter wear, for the inside of Cobalt Gorge was kept warm, insulated by the canyon walls and a thick manufactured steam cloud overhead.

"You don't have to wear one," Rylin said. "But those shorts and bare feet won't do much to keep you warm."

Obbin sighed. "Your sewing could use some work." He smiled at his brother.

"Ha, I did my best. It's not like I could ask our mother or sisters for help," he said. "Might cause some suspicion on how I came by the furs and why I needed warm clothing."

"So we could play hunt each other," Obbin teased. "We are known for our big imaginations." Obbin pulled a leaf that had already begun to change colors from a nearby branch. "Already the green disappears."

"Be patient, brother. The leaves and plants will grow again," Rylin said. "Remember the ancient Scripture, 'Behold, I am doing a new thing; now it springs forth, do you not perceive it? I will make a way in the wilderness and rivers in the desert.' "

Obbin nodded. Their father, the king, often read from the ancient books in the palace library. "I guess. But I don't think that's what that passage meant."

Rylin shrugged.

Shaboom, crack! Thunder rumbled overhead.

"Wow that was close. It's coming quicker than I expected," Rylin said. "We shouldn't be in the tree anymore."

But Obbin didn't respond. He raised his arm and pointed. "Look, Rylin. It's a . . . a ship. And it's in trouble."

A silver spaceship tumbled end over end in the air. A streak of lightning blasted into the side of it, emitting a shower of blue sparks. The ship was going to crash. Obbin stared in amazement, Rylin at his side. The storm's danger was momentarily forgotten.

Seconds later the ship straightened out from its uncontrolled rotation and turned toward the brothers. Relief coursed over Obbin.

"We'd better get back," Rylin said. "We can't have them seeing us."

"Why?" Obbin asked.

"It's our responsibility as princes of the royal family," Rylin reminded his brother. "We have to protect the secrecy of the *Blauwe Mensen*. If these intruders find us out here, they might—"

"—tell someone they saw blue kids in the forest," Obbin finished. "You know the local legends; we are just a myth to the people in the city. We don't exist."

The brothers watched the silver ship stop in midair and begin descending into the forest. It'd landed not too far from them. Had they already been seen?

"You can run away if you want," Obbin said. "I want to see the ship, and whoever is on it."

Rylin shook his head. "Suit yourself, but I'm not getting in trouble for this."

"Nobody's going to get in trouble," Obbin scoffed. He was far too clever to be caught by anybody on that ship.

Rylin moved to the ladder. "If you don't return by night fall, then I'll have to tell father."

"I'll be back way before then," Obbin said. "I'll be back before the snow begins to fall."

Rylin snorted. "Right."

The brothers began their descent from the tree house. At the base, Rylin used a loose vine and pulley to tug the rope ladder back into place. Then he tucked the vine against the tree and it nearly disappeared from view. It was well camouflaged.

"Are you sure you won't come with?" Rylin asked.

Obbin reached out his hand, and took his brothers. "I must bid you farewell," he said in his deepest voice. "If I should not return from this mission, you were my favorite brother." Then he turned and without another word ran off into the woods. He was in pursuit of the silver ship.

FIRST SIGHT

Obbin stood behind the trunk of a willow tree on the edge of the clearing. Its long tendrils swished back and forth around him, further shielding him from view. The silvery ship sat in the center of the clearing. A word etched onto the bow of it read, *Phoenix*.

He'd tried knocking on a hatch earlier, but no one responded. He waited and waited; finally resolving to sit against one of the trees at the edge of the forest to watch.

He had a good view of the ship from there. The sky had grown darker, the air colder. He could hear acorns crashing down from the Oak trees in the forest.

He hoped they would come out soon. Otherwise this whole mission would have been a waste. Obbin needed to make a trade with the spaceship's passengers, or at least meet them so he had something to show for his efforts.

There was a *swoosh* and a hatch on the side of the ship slid up. Obbin jumped. A sandy-haired boy about Obbin's age dashed out. Obbin twisted and rolled to the backside of the tree. The boy hadn't seen him, he'd been too busy sealing the hatch. The sandy-haired boy ran toward the back of the ship, and started up a ladder.

Whoosh! The hatch flew open a second time, and another boy, identical to the first, ran from the ship. But he stopped almost immediately. He gazed up at the pillars of trees all around. The boy stepped back. The very first time Rylin and Obbin snuck out from the gorge, Obbin himself had been amazed at the size of the trees.

Obbin realized he looked just like the boy who'd climbed up on to the ship. Obbin looked up. The first kid stood up on the silver ship, staring down at the other. He wore a mischievous grin on his face. Obbin darted behind another tree trunk to get a better look.

A howl whistled from the fir trees as the wind slipped through the pine needles. The boy near the door jumped back.

"Ha, ha!" laughed the first boy.

The second spun around.

The first chuckled again. "You look a little scared, Mason," the first boy said.

"I am not," Mason called back.

"Sure you aren't." the other teased.

The wind howled, halting the banter between the two boys. Obbin needed to make his move now if he was going to meet the boys and see the ship. He had pondered asking for a ride on the spaceship, but there was no time for that. The storm was nearly on top of them. Maybe he could at least trade for something. Get a souvenir to prove to Rylin that he'd actually spoken to them; which he hadn't done yet.

"How bout we call a—a truce?" the boy atop the ship asked. Obbin could hear a growing anxiety in his voice. This kid wasn't as brave as he'd tried to appear.

"Fair enough," agreed Mason.

"Smell the fresh air, Mason," suggested the first boy. He stretched his arms out. "We've been stuck in the ship since early this morning. Let's enjoy the outdoors."

"Sure, but how'd you get up there?" asked Mason.

The boy atop the *Phoenix* pointed. "There's a service ladder on back. Hurry, I'll help you."

The boy named Mason started toward the rear of the ship. He was doing something, but Obbin couldn't quite see what. Obbin moved around the trunk of his tree, and ran to the next over for a better angle.

"Whoa!" screamed Mason, the boy nearly fell over. Obbin ducked back behind the tree. His bare back pressed against the rough bark. Obbin started to look around the tree again. Why had he been startled? He wanted to meet them.

He started forward, then the wind howled loudly and something snapped in the forest behind him. And instead of exposing himself to Mason, he darted behind another tree. He'd moved closer to the ship. But if they were like him they might be armed with slingshots, or maybe something worse.

"Austin, did you see that?" Mason called out.

Austin's words were lost to the wind. Obbin looked toward them again. He slipped from tree trunk to tree trunk.

Both boys were at the back of the *Phoenix*, Mason halfway up the ladder. Atop he pointed toward the tree Obbin had been behind. Clearly they didn't know how quickly Obbin could move. Closer now, he could hear them again. They seemed to be scouring the tree line. But they wouldn't find him over there. If he was hunting them, they'd already be his captives. This was a serious boost to his confidence. There was nothing to be afraid of.

"I don't see anything Mason. Is this a joke?"

A joke? Obbin was no joke, and it was time to introduce himself.

The willow branches twisted in the growing wind. "I saw something, I know I did," Mason countered.

"It was probably just an animal," Austin said. But he sounded unsure. "It's probably more scared of us than we are of it."

Suddenly the face of Austin appeared peering over the back of the ship. Obbin smiled, but it wasn't well received. The boy's face disappeared, and Obbin heard a series of thumps on the metal topside of the ship. The noise echoed in the forest all around, like a warning to any animals that'd not burrowed in for the winter yet.

"What—what did you see?" Obbin heard Mason ask.

"I don't know—it was blue—," Austin said.

Obbin smiled to himself at the statement. He was indeed blue. He doubted many people outside his gorge had ever seen a blue person before. He'd been told that most humans weren't blue. And from what he and Rylin had seen on their adventures this was true. They'd seen many earth-tone colors of skin, but never blue.

"—it looked human," Austin finished.

Obbin couldn't hold back a laugh, of course he was human.

"Human?" he heard Mason ask as the wind erupted into another chorus of howls.

He would show them he was human once he climbed atop this ladder.

"What should we do?" Austin continued.

"I don't know!"

These two are ridiculous, thought Obbin. If it were him and Rylin they'd be standing up to fight. They wouldn't have been scared. Obbin took hold of the bottom rung. He heard a clank as an acorn fell from a nearby branch.

"Do you see anything?" he head Mason ask.

"No" was Austin's only reply.

It was time to end their suspense, they'd see him soon enough. Obbin took the ladder quickly, but slowed himself before peeking over. He wanted to be sure they'd not armed themselves with the giant acorn. Obbin had been hit with one before, leaving a serious bruise on his leg. He wasn't about to take one to the head.

"Hello," he said as he popped his head into view. No acorn in hand. The two boys were huddled together a short way down the top side of the ship. They looked quite frightened.

NEW FRIENDS

The boys started to whisper, but Obbin could read their lips.

"It...he spoke," Mason half mouthed, half whispered.

"And in our language," replied Austin.

"My name's Obbin," Obbin greeted and extended his hand toward the twins.

Austin nudged his brother. "Mason, say something."

"H-hello," Mason stammered. He slowly got to his feet, holding out his hand as if showing Obbin he was not dangerous.

Obbin shook his head at the peculiarity. "Are you guys all right?"

"Yeah, ummm, I'm Mason, and this…this is Austin, my twin."

That made complete sense, though he did see one difference; something about their eyes. Different colors, one of the boys had blue and the other green.

Obbin climbed all the way on the ship. He could almost feel the boys' eyes scanning every part of his body. He softly flexed his muscles and tightened his abs. He didn't mind their stares, knowing they hadn't seen a blue person with green hair before. But it also gave him a chance to position himself as strong and a reasonable challenge, should they try to capture him or something.

"He looks like a boy. Like a human boy, I mean," Mason whispered.

"But he's blue!"

"I know."

The obvious statements and the notion that he couldn't hear their discussion made him smile. He approached, hands out to show he wasn't armed at the moment. "Nice to meet you, but I can't stay long. I was out in the woods when I saw your ship land." Obbin was careful not to mention Rylin.

Mason scratched his head. "You saw us?"

"Yeah. Lots of ships fly over the forest, but very few try to land in it. I figured you guys may have crashed," Obbin said.

"We almost did," admitted Austin truthfully.

Obbin looked around at the dark woods. More leaves flittered to the ground. "Well, I can't stay long. There's a storm moving in."

Mason looked up.

"I knocked on the door earlier, but you never answered. I've been out here for a while," Obbin explained. "I was about to leave when you" —Obbin pointed to Austin— "came rushing out the door."

"I didn't see you," Austin said.

"You only see me if I want you to see me," Obbin boasted. "It's too bad you didn't come earlier. I wanted to show you something."

"What?" Austin asked.

"I guess there's still time." Obbin reached into his pocket and pulled out a crystal. "Here, look at this." The expressions on the boys' faces made it clear they'd never seen anything like it. For Obbin it wasn't a big deal; his home was littered with jewels.

Mason took the crystal and held it close. "Wow!" His brother peered over his shoulder.

"You like it?" Obbin said, moving closer to the boys. "Then let's trade."

Mason looked up but was silent.

"Do you want to trade?" Obbin asked impatiently as he heard a peal of distant thunder. Time was running out.

"Sure," Mason said, staring at the jewel. "Have whatever you want."

That was all he needed to hear. Obbin moved passed the double tailfin of the *Pheonix* and down the ladder.

He heard Austin over his shoulder. "Can I hold it?"

"In a minute," was the reply he heard Mason give.

"Give it to me!" he heard Austin shout.

"No!"

He and his brothers wrestled over things all the time. But Obbin certainly hadn't meant to cause a fight. A crackle of thunder reminded him of the coming storm. He slipped in through the open cargo bay door.

The first thing that caught his eye was some sort of scooter thing. He'd seen people from the shiny dome city riding through the woods on them before. This one however looked broken. There were possibly hundreds of crates stacked along the backside of the bay. He felt the excitement rising in his chest. There were so many crates to choose from, if only he knew what was in them.

Obbin would just have to take his chances.

OBBIN'S PRIZE

Obbin opened one of the large crates and began digging through it. Bingo. This crate contained several bright orange articles of clothing, space suits perhaps. Rylin wouldn't be able to doubt the success of his mission, or say the risk hadn't been worth it.

These boys certainly have a lot of cool things, Obbin thought.

Just then the twins rushed into the *Phoenix*. "Nice ship!" Obbin commented.

Austin rushed toward him, "No, no, don't touch anything."

Obbin ignored him and kept digging. He pulled one from the crate that looked like it might be his size. He held it against his body. "I think this will fit."

"Put that back," Mason said.

"You took the crystal; I take the suit," Obbin said, starting for the door. "It's only fair."

The twins paused and looked at each other. Obbin knew he'd better get out of there quickly, before the boys changed their minds. He needed the suit to show his brother as proof. If the boys decided not to trade, then he'd be left with nothing. Besides, he was running out of time. The storm was about to hit. Obbin dashed out the door and took off toward the trail. He looked back to see the twins charge out.

It's a fair trade, Obbin thought. *I must get home.* He slipped into the woods and ran. The path was narrow and slightly overgrown by Starlight plants.

The trail sloped down and the ground rose on either side of him, creating a trench. A clap of thunder silenced the busy chorus of creatures, who'd yet found their burrows or enough stored food. Obbin looked back and didn't see the twins, but he continued to hurry along just in case. The star-shaped leaves of the Starlight plants were now a ceiling overhead.

"There he is!" one of the twins cried out. The shout startled Obbin, and he darted forward, nearly dropping his prize trade. He looked back, the twins were sprinting. With each curve, Obbin noticed the boys were gaining on him. He just needed to make it to the crevice.

Obbin broke out of the trench and onto a wide dirt path. The soldiers of his village often used it for their patrols. Obbin looked back, he couldn't see the boys. But he knew they were coming.

Just as he charged back onto the continuation of his narrow dirt path, he heard Austin. "We've got him now!"

These boys are fast, Obbin thought. At least he didn't have much further to go.

The leaves of the Starlight plants had begun to glow, the night was coming. Thunder rumbled overhead. So was the storm.

Obbin picked up his pace. He ducked under fallen limbs and jumped over ferns. The sound of rushing air grew louder, but it wasn't from the storm. Then the path turned sharply and dropped downward. He'd gotten to the rocky clearing. Ahead of him was a wall of rising blue steam; behind it his home.

"Look! There he is!" cried out one of the boys.

Obbin ran for the thick, blue cloud and disappeared into it, though he imagined the orange spacesuit might not hide as well in the steam as his bare skin. Still, he immediately slowed knowing the crevice was just a short ways in. Though he'd done this a thousand times, he still had to be careful, or risk falling into the lava filled gorge.

ONE WRONG MOVE

Obbin deftly located the top of the ladder and started down.

He heard the twins slow their pace. "Hold on! Do you hear that?"

Obbin remained completely still at the bottom of the ladder. Over the driving sound of the rising blue steam, he could hear the boys' heavy breathing.

"We can't...just run into...that cloud...we have no idea...what or who...is behind it." He head Mason say.

"Yeah...but he's...getting away!" Austin argued.

And he had. *I've beaten the boys,* Obbin thought with some pride. He held up the orange suit and smiled, then up through the spotty steam. The purple clouds were overhead, but no rain or snow had yet begun to fall. *And I've beaten the storm. Rylin was always worried about dangerous "what-ifs" that never happened.*

Obbin took off across the three-vine bridge, the orange suit slung over his shoulder. It wobbled back and forth, but no more than he was used to.

"Whoa!" he screamed as his right foot slipped off the foot-vine. He swung his arm to balance himself, but the bridge bounced from his hurried movements. In the next moment, Obbin's entire body dangled by one hand. His other held the orange suit.

Obbin strained to pull himself up, but it was too hard with only one hand. He'd have to let go of the orange suit, the one thing he had to prove his meeting with the spaceship passengers. It was an item unlike anything he'd ever been able to acquire. There was nothing like it in his entire valley. It didn't matter that he could only share it with one person, his brother; this was a treasure.

Now he'd have to let it fall into the magma river below. There'd be no chance of getting it back. It would melt in the molten rock.

"Hold on!" a familiar voice cried.

Obbin looked toward the voice. Rylin! His brother stepped out from an opening in the cliff at the far side of the chasm. His older brother carefully but quickly started across the bridge. Hope flooded through Obbin. He redoubled his grip on the vine while holding tight to the orange suit.

Rylin moved closer, then grabbed Obbin's arm. "I've got you." Obbin's feet found the rope.

Obbin ducked his head. "Thanks. I was foolish to go off alone."

"I should've stayed with you," Rylin admitted once his brother was safe. Lightning streaked the sky, followed by an ear splitting crack of thunder. "We'd better go," Rylin said.

The two brothers slowly crossed the rest of the way. Obbin looked over his shoulder to see if the twins had come through at all. "I met the ship's pilots. They were kids just like me."

Rylin shook his head. "Like you?"

Obbin handed his brother the orange space suit, as they stepped into the entry of the tunnel. "See it's some sort of space suit and it's my size."

Rylin rolled his eyes. "You want me to believe that two kids flew that huge silver ship."

"It's called the *Phoenix*," Obbin said. "And yes, the only people there were two boys my height."

Obbin's older brother sighed. "It won't be easy sneaking this through town and into the castle."

"We'll figure it out," Obbin said. He patted Rylin on the back. "You should have come with me. You'd have liked it. It was a great adventure."

"I'm sure it was," Rylin admitted. "And you're right. I shouldn't have let you go alone. You could have been captured, or hurt."

"Or killed."

"You almost were."

"So it was your fault?" Obbin said laughing.

"No," Rylin answered, trying not to smile. "That's not what I was saying. But if you go on anymore adventures, I'm going with you."

Obbin placed the metal grate back into place at the hole of the tunnel. The bridge was a secret to all but him and his brother. The tunnel that led to it seemed like nothing more than a drain. They had a long way to go through the caverns that lead to their gorge.

Obbin took a deep breath. His adventure was certainly exciting, and he hoped it'd be enough to satisfy his appetite until the thaw more than a year from now.

ABOUT
BROCK EASTMAN

Brock Eastman likes to write, but his main focus is on his family. They reside at the base of America's mountain, and are learning to call Colorado home. However, they sometimes need to visit the comfortable cornfields and hospitality of the Midwest, especially during the harvest.

Brock is Product Marketing Manager at Focus on the Family, where he has the privilege to work on the world renowned Adventures in Odyssey brand, a show his dad got him hooked on when he was little boy.

He started writing The Quest for Truth series in 2005 and 5 years later, with his wife's encouragement, signed a publishing deal. In that same year he signed 2 additional contracts, giving him 9 books releasing in 2.5 years. YIKES! He's always thinking of his next story and totes a thumb-drive full of ideas.

His favorite Bible verse is Ephesians 4:32.

What people are saying

The Quest for Truth:

"The Wikks are regular kids given a Galactic size challenge. Readers will follow Oliver, Tiffany, and twins, Mason and Austin as they trek through eerie catacombs, mysterious ruins, and creepy castles that defy imagination. One part Indiana Jones, a handful of Swiss Family Robinson, and some Intergalactic excitement, the Quest for Truth is a riveting tale of just how far mankind will go for the ultimate prize."
- Wayne Thomas Batson, best-selling author of The Door Within Trilogy, The Berinfell Prophecies, and The Dark Sea Annals

"Don't even touch this book unless you plan to read it at once. Taken wastes no time thrusting its readers headlong into the beginning of what promises to be an epic saga. Exploding with mystery and high-stakes adventure, this book is masterfully crafted to awaken even the most stubborn of imaginations. And yet perhaps the most impressive feat is Mr. Eastman's ability to punctuate all of it with a deep and powerful message of faith. A job well done."
- Christopher Miller, coauthor of the multi-award-winning Codebearers series

"Taken is a fast-paced, fun, easy-to-read book. It allowed my imagination and mind to get lost in the story. I enjoyed it and can't wait to read the next Quest for Truth book!"
- Brooke Harrell, age 13, CO

"I can not wait for risk to come out. I loved taken I read it over and over again when I can."
- Caleb Frey, age 11, IL

"My buddy Brock Eastman has a winner here! Take fascinating characters, put them on a fantastical adventure, and tell the story at a page-turning pace, and you've got Taken, the first volume of his forthcoming, five-book series titled The Quest for Truth. Oh, and parents, don't forget his solid emphasis on Christian principles. Tell you what: get this book for your kids, and they'll enjoy it so much that I bet you'll end up reading it too! Way to go Brock!"
- Frank Pastore, host of The Frank Pastore Show on KKLA 99.5 FM in Los Angeles, Author of Shattered: Struck Down, But Not Destroyed

"I'm constantly on the lookout for books that are exciting, but not too scary for my school aged children. Eastman consistently delivers action packed page turners that are not only a joy for the whole family to read, but also strengthen our spiritual walks."
-Elissa Peterson, OH, Mom of 4, creator of Don't Let Life Pass You By blog

"Sit back and let Brock take you on an exciting journey to the far reaches of the galaxy that explores the meaning of family and friends"
- Mark Redekop, of the Adventures in Odyssey Wiki

"Taken is awesome! People of any age will enjoy it. I can't wait for the rest of the series!"
- Ruth Santoyo, age 14, MO
"The Wikks' adventures kept me at the edge of my seat throughout the whole book!"
- Cody Lugovskiy, age 13, CA

"The book kept me very interested and I was really excited when I got to read it! It was one of the best books I've ever read. I would definitely recommend it!"
- Nicole Blunier, age 10, IL

"Finally, something new, exciting, and original! Brock Eastman has written a page-turner that will definitely make you want to read the sequel."
- Jonathan Maiocco, age 17, GA

"The Quest for Truth is a riveting tale of four young kids who have to learn to help and rely on each other. With lives on the line, courage, wit, companionship, and teamwork are vital for Oliver, Tiffany, Austin, and Mason. This book stole my time away as I continued to turn the pages. Next one, please!"
- Hannah Davis, age 14, TN

"Taken is a fast paced action adventures book that I couldn't put down! It was well written and easy to read and each chapter gets better than the last! I can't wait for the rest in the series."
- Michael Wilmot, age 14, Western Australia.

"It got right to the adventure, which was good in my opinion. It wasn't hard to figure out what was going on, the beginning was easy to understand. I think you should read it. Watch out for the Übel!"
- Alex Peterson, age 9, OH

"Good, clean, adventures, Christian fiction set in a future time period to reveal truth as to man's origin and over come evil is the bases of this Taken. From the start, this book sends you into adventure and mystery of the Wikk siblings. The sci-fi within the story, like the ships that travel from one planet to another and the mysterious blue people, will remind readers of Star Wars yet the series is set to bring Christian truths into the mix. You are left with the hint of many exciting things to happen in the future of this series."
- Rachel Harris, age 21, MN

Sages of Darkness:

"Taylor is an average boy, with unaverage abilities. Sages of Darkness reveals the evil around us, but uncovers the strength in all of us. With pulse pounding action, the Sages of Darkness trilogy will keep you up all night reading, which is a good thing since you won't want to turn out the lights."
- Wayne Thomas Batson, best-selling author of The Door Within Trilogy, The Berinfell Prophecies, and The Dark Sea Annals

"A highly entertaining read and a unique story, Howlsage is sure to leave a positive impression on discerning young adult Christian readers. This story is not for the faint of heart; it is quite literally the battle between humanity and demons who've taken physical form. Brock Eastman has written a keeper you will dread to read, but can't help finishing! I look forward to the next installment in this series."
-Scott Appleton, author of The Sword of the Dragon series

"When you meet author Brock Eastman, you are bathed in energy, optimism, enthusiasm, and a genuine reflection of Christ's love for His people. When you read his book, HowlSage, you are immersed in a tale of adventure, drama, action, and matters of eternal consequence. Join Taylor, Jesse, and Ike as they learn how to defeat evil in the form of the wicked sages."
- Donita K. Paul, author of the Dragon Keeper Chronicles

"BlizzardSage is now one of my favorite books! I love the characters
and the lessons about Christianity."
- Ryan Matlock, age 14, IN

"Our house is jam packed with books, but my nine year old snatched up Howl Sage and disappeared with it. I've never seen her this excited about a book. The book never left her hand until it was done, and she woke up at six in the morning, snuck into the bathroom and read in there until the rest of the family woke up. Now she's pestering me constantly to read Blizzard Sage which, as of right now, isn't out yet! Hurry release the next book! Our family loves the Sages of Darkness series and we can't wait to see what happens next!"
- Matt Mikalatos, author of My Imaginary Jesus and Night of the Living Dead Christian

"BlizzardSage is an action-packed roller coaster of a book. It lived up to and surpassed the expectations I had for it after reading HowlSage--I couldn't turn the pages fast enough. Brock Eastman will have to pull out all the gadgets he's got up his sleeves if he hopes to top this one."
-Christian Miles, author of The Scarlet Key

"I'm constantly on the lookout for books that are exciting, but not too scary for my school aged children. Eastman consistently delivers action packed page turners that are not only a joy for the whole family to read, but also strengthen our spiritual walks."
-Elissa Peterson, OH, Mom of 4, creator of Don't Let Life Pass You By blog

"I liked all the different locations that the characters traveled to, but the last one was my favorite. It was just as good as HowlSage."
- Alex Peterson, age 9, OH

"Work couldn't get over soon enough each day. The book [HowlSage] was waiting."
- Colin Knapp, Age 22, IL

"I was totally immersed in the fight between good and evil that unfolded in HowlSage. The spiritual struggles that Tyler endures, makes him an easily identifiable comrade to the reader. You find yourself cheering him on and holding your breath as danger unfolds. The cliff hanging ending of HowlSage left me frantically turning the last few pages, crying out no, no, no... just a little more...Absolutely cannot wait till the next book in the Sages of Darkness series, BlizzardSage, is released so Tyler can continue the good fight!"
- Lisa Wiegand, IL, Teacher

"HowlSage definitely a bit of a hit. My son's not going to bed. Seems this book is head and shoulders above any he's read in a while. Well done!"
- Angela Wilmot, Western Australia, Mom of 7

"A clever blend of Percy Jackson and Fablehaven, HowlSage kept me up all night reading. Full of suspense, action, and gadgets-- readers will cheer for young Taylor as he hunts down demons and discovers the life he's supposed to lead. Two thumbs up."
- Christian Miles, age 17, WI

"Thrilling chases, advanced technology, solid friendships, and spiritual warfare; Howlsage is absolutely brimming with adventure! It's also told in a way that younger kids can understand and relate to. I have 5 younger siblings and the youngest is only 6. I know how hard it is to find books that grab their interests and hold their attentions, but that also have good Christian values and Biblical principles that they can understand. Not only did I enjoy reading Howlsage as an adult, but I know that my younger brothers and sisters will love this book as well. I can hardly wait to read it to them!"
-Nichole White, age 22, IL

"Thrilling events and vivid descriptions of characters made me feel as if I was right there fighting evil with Taylor and his friends! You won't want to put the book down until you've read the last page."
- Larisa Kolmyk, age 22, CA

"HowlSage was terrifying, in the kind of way that makes your heart leap up into your throat, preventing you from shouting, 'Mommy, SAVE ME!' You'll sweat along with Taylor as he forges through the grey mist, or shiver with Ike, swinging in a cage in the darkness.
It was endearing. Not the HowlSage, (see top,) but the other characters of the book. Taylor was a warrior, willing to fight the good fight. Ike was a student with an open mind, and a child of the Lord. Jesse was smart-mouthed; witty, but keeping a dark secret.
And, in its entirety, HowlSage was gripping, holding my attention as raptly as I held its pages. Flip. Flip. Flip. This soft, papery soundtrack accompanied my reading late into the night, picking up speed as I went. HowlSage was the first in a series that is bound to get better and better with every new book."
- Seth Skogerboe, age 13 Plymouth, MN

"HowlSage is an exciting and thrilling ride; it is a must read for all people my age and older!! HowlSage took me under 24 hours to read and my literally eyes were glued to it! It was brilliantly and amazingly written and I can't explain in words how amazing this book is! I can't wait for the rest in the series!!"
-Michael Wilmot, age 14, Western Australia.

"HowlSage is an exceptionally well written book that kept me on my toes the whole time. I can barely contain my excitement to read BlizzardSage."
- Hannah Frey, age 16, IL

"I loved HowlSage! It was fun and exciting. You never knew what would happen next. If BlizzardSage is half as good, it will be AMAZING! I can hardly wait to read it."
- Aaron Frey, age 14, IL

"Sages of Darkness is the next Ya Series for this generation, better than the epic series Percy Jackson and Harry Potter. It's a must read for all ages!"
- Solomon Stone, age 17, WA

"It was fast paced. I thought the beginning of the book was a little confusing because I didn't know exactly what was going on, but the more I read, the more I understood. This book is not as scary as it looks based on the cover. I thought it was a good book."
- Alex Peterson, age 9, OH

"It's yummerful!"
- Allie Mikalatos, age 9, WA

Made in the USA
San Bernardino, CA
11 April 2015